Sammi Jo and the Best Adventure Ever!

Maya Reese, and Reese, Have Fun! Dede Stockton

Sammi Jo Adventure Series
Book 3

Sammi Jo
and the
Best Adventure Ever!

Dede Stockton

Illustrations and Cover Design
Gaspar Sabater
Professional Illustrator and Cartoonist

DREAMMAKER BOOKS LLC / CENTENNIAL, CO

Dede Stockton/DreamMaker Books LLC
PO 461545
Aurora, CO 80016

www.sammijoadventures.com
www.dreammakerbook.com
www.dedestockton.com

Publisher's Note: This is a work of fiction. Names, characters, places, and incidents, are a product of the author's imagination. Locales and public names are sometimes used for atmospheric purposes. Any resemblance to actual people, living or dead, or to businesses, companies, events, institutions, or locales is completely coincidental.

Book design © 2017 BookDesignTemplates.com

Cover Design and Illustrations - Gaspar Sabater <gasparsabater@gmail.com>

Ordering Information: Special discounts are available on quantity purchases by corporations, associations, and others. For details, contact the publisher at the address above.

Sammi Jo and the Best Adventure Ever / Dede Stockton

ISBN (paperback): 978-0-9987102-7-3

ISBN (Ebook): 978-0-9987102-8-0

ISBN (audio book): 978-0-9987102-9-7

Library of Congress Control Number: 2017916961

Lexile® measure: 890L

Printed in the United States of America

Sammi Jo and the
Best Adventure Ever

is dedicated to my parents
Who showed me the world and opened my
mind to different people and cultures!

Darold Knutson – 1930 - 2001

Vivian Knutson – 1927 - 2017

Contents

List of New Characters

Dragon names:

Drakon

Zurka – Drakon's Brother

Lyzer – Drakon's Brother

Kyree – Drakon's Sister

Lurko and Maximus – 2 dragons found by Kyree

Ghost Parrots:

Petey, Percy, Nellie and Minnie

Wayward Merman – Tekoah

His horse: Saqua

Sea turtle: Arkeo

Dolphin: Echo

Names of new children

Jase and Riley – Dog is Jack

1

What Day Is It?

Sammi Jo's eyes popped open!

What day is it? Is today my birthday? No, it's not until next week, but I feel certain that something awesome is going to happen today! I wonder what it is?

Sammi Jo was used to getting these feelings that something great was going to happen. And it usually did. Whether she was just lucky or if it was because she always tried to look at the bright side of things, we will never know, but she did always seem to have the best days ever and did always try to find the bright side of things, so perhaps something special would happen today!

Yesterday was such a special day at the adventure that Sammi Jo couldn't imagine anything better than that, but her new friends had promised her so much

more to come... so she would just have to wait and see what was in store for today and the days to come!

In the last week she had met stingrays, mermaids, mermen and seahorses. She had seen music playing fish and watched mermen riding scary looking bull sharks and cowfish. She had even gotten to ride a stingray!

Today they would be going to back to Edenlandia to visit – so who knows what could happen today.

Sammi Jo continued to lay in bed daydreaming for a while, until she heard Jake pounding on her door.

"Wakeup, sleepyhead!" he roared as the pounding increased, "I thought that I was the lazy one! Get up, get up, get up!"

Sammi Jo rolled out of bed quickly and went running to the door!

"Jeez, Jake, you're going to break my door down if you don't stop! What are you in such a hurry about?"

"Well," Jake grinned, "you are usually the one coaxing me out of bed early, so I thought I would return the favor. Aren't you anxious to get back to Edenlandia? I thought that Screech was picking us up early again."

"Okay, okay. I'm hurrying, I was just day dreaming about what could possibly top the adventure. But, even if there is nothing special planned – it will be awesome just being there with them!"

She hurried to brush her teeth and get dressed, wondering all the time what would be in store for them today.

She was so intent on trying to guess what it was that it took her several moments to realize that her shell phone was ringing.

"Hi!" she said breathlessly into the phone.

"Where are you?" asked Screech. "I have been waiting here forever!"

"Okay, okay!" Sammi Jo laughed. "Hold onto your horses, we will be there soon!"

And then she raced down the stairs to the kitchen as fast as she could!

2

Awesome News!

By the time Sammi Jo had made it down to the kitchen, Jake was talking excitedly to someone on the kitchen telephone.

"Who is Jake talking to?" asked Sammi Jo.

"His brother called to talk with him," answered her mom.

Sammi Jo sat down quietly at the table and began to eat her cereal while staring sadly into her bowl. I sure wish I had a brother or sister. I have lots of friends and a wonderful family, but it would be so nice to be able to have someone that I can share everything with... Someone that goes on all of our family vacations, can share the same stories, someone that can be at school with me...

"What's going on in your head?" asked her mom.

"Oh, not much," sighed Sammi Jo, "I was just wishing that I had a brother or sister like Jake and Kara and all of my other friends."

"So, you still want some siblings, huh?" answered mom. "Dad and I thought that maybe you weren't interested in that anymore since we haven't heard you mention it in a while."

"I think about it all the time, but don't want to make you and dad feel bad, so I just don't talk about it."

"Well," said Sammi Jo's mom, "your dad and I talk about having more children, too. We wondered if it would upset you or if you enjoyed getting all of the attention all of the time."

"Oh, no! I mean, don't get me wrong, I love getting all of the attention, but I'm pretty certain that you and dad have plenty of love to spread around and I am willing to share!"

"We have talked about it quite a bit," replied her mom, "but, have decided that we are simply not interested in having a baby. We are way too busy and I don't want to stop travelling, which I would have to do if we were to have a baby."

"So, you are not interested in having any more children?" asked Sammi Jo sadly.

"No," smiled her mom, "we are simply not interested in having a baby."

"What do you mean by that?" inquired Sammi Jo.

"There are a lot of children out there who need a family," explained her mom, "for many reasons. We have actually talked to an adoption agency about the possibility of adopting a child that desperately needs a family to love."

"Seriously?" asked Sammi Jo in disbelief. "You have actually talked about this? Why haven't you told me?"

"We wanted to make sure that we would be able to handle it all before we talked to you about it."

"What's going on?" asked Jake.

He had been off the phone for a couple of minutes now and just gotten in on the tail end of the conversation.

"My folks are talking about adopting a child!" squealed Sammi Jo in delight! "Isn't that AWESOME!"

"What? Really? That is so totally cool!" exclaimed Jake. "When is this going to happen?"

"Well, now that I know Sammi Jo is okay with the whole idea. We can call and let them know that we are ready to go ahead!" said Sammi Jo's mom with a big grin. "I can't wait to tell your dad when he gets home." She said to Sammi Jo.

"Yeah! Me too!" laughed Sammi Jo with delight!

"He went into town to get some supplies and do some research at the library, but we will tell him all about our conversation at dinner tonight," explained

Mrs. Meriwether. "So, you two can go ahead and get started on your plans for today and we will talk about this again later."

"But, Mom..." Sammi Jo began.

"No more talk about this until your dad gets home," Mrs. Meriwether stated firmly. "He would not want to miss out on all of this excitement!"

"Okay," agreed Sammi Jo with a smile. "But, it is the very first thing we will talk about, right?"

"Absolutely!" said her mom with a smile. "Pinky promise?" she continued as she held out her pinky finger to Sammi Jo.

Sammi Jo extended her pinky finger as they solemnly shook on their promise and then Mrs. Meriwether waved good bye as she headed up to her office and Sammi Jo and Jake headed out the back door to see what Screech had planned for them today!

3

What's Happening?

Sammi Jo ran breathlessly up the beach with her arms spread wide, spinning and twirling in excitement!

"I can't believe it! I can't believe it!" she squealed over and over again.

"Better slow down," cautioned Jake, "You don't know how soon this is going to happen. It could be years!"

"I won't believe that it will be years – I want this too bad! You don't know what it is like being alone all the time. YOU have a brother! The only time I get to have other kids around is when someone is visiting. I want to have other kids around all the time!"

"Be careful what you wish for," moaned Jake, "I would love to have some 'alone' time. My little brother is ALWAYS around and sometimes I seriously wish he would just disappear."

"Oh, you don't mean that," admonished Sammi Jo. "If he weren't there you would miss him terribly."

"Maybe ..." questioned Jake, "but, once in a while ... it would be nice!"

They had arrived at their beach by this time and were both standing, breathlessly, looking for Screech.

It didn't take long before they saw his big smiling face pop up by the rock and they quickly put on their breathing masks and their translators and jumped into the water.

"Beat you there!" Sammi Jo hollered as she began churning the water rapidly to reach Screech first.

"Right behind you!" Jake yelled back.

They both arrived at the same time and struggled to climb up on Screeches back as they laughed hysterically!

"What are you two so excited about today?" questioned Screech.

Sammi Jo began to tell him excitedly about her news as they dove into the water. Screech, of all 'people,' would certainly understand as he was an only child himself.

"Well, that is certainly cool," he responded as she reached the end of her story. "It would be awesome to have a brother or a sister. I doubt that will ever happen for me, but I have plenty of folks to keep me company in Edenlandia!"

This was being said as he slowed down at the perimeter of Edenlandia. Things seemed a little strange today. Everyone was quiet, and they weren't greeted by the swarms of merchildren like they normally were.

"What's happening?" whispered Sammi Jo. "Things seem really quiet today."

Sammi Jo and Jake glanced around nervously trying to see if they could see anything odd

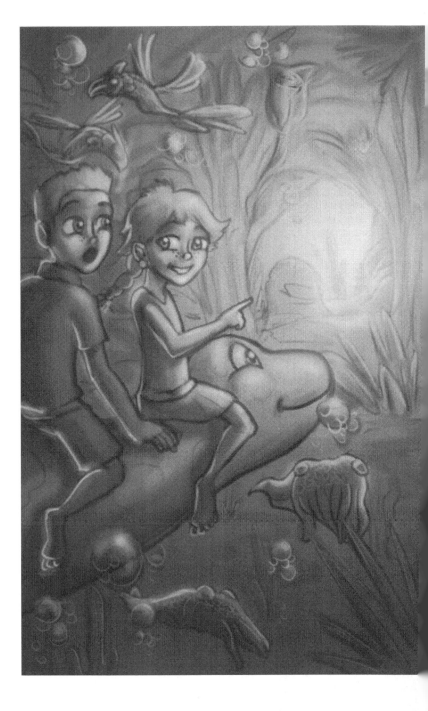

happening, but all they could see was a much larger gathering of dragonfly fish than were normally there. It seemed as if they were nervous as they darted quickly back and forth around the perimeters of the little village of Edenlandia. The ocean floor was also covered with tiny little cuttlefish, crawling along on their little front legs and camouflaged to blend in perfectly with the sand.

"We are not quite sure," said Screech, "but, as you can see, the dragonfly fish and the cuttlefish are acting odd and their nervousness is definitely effecting everyone's mood."

Kirstin came gliding up at that moment to greet them. She seemed very subdued and was glancing nervously over her shoulder as if she was afraid something was going to grab her.

"Good Morning!" she greeted with her warm smile. "It is so nice to see you both again!"

"You, too!" replied Jake and Sammi Jo together.

"What's going on?" questioned Sammi Jo. "It seems crazy quiet here today."

"The dragonfly fish are acting oddly and because they guard our land, we are concerned about what is happening, or what may happen." Replied Kirstin in a hushed voice. "The last time this happened was hundreds of years ago. Long before any of us were born, but the stories have passed down through the generations and we are all very concerned."

"Stories about what?" questioned Sammi Jo.

"Let's go and greet the others and then we will tell you all about it." Kirstin responded as she motioned for them to follow and then glided silently toward one of the large caves.

Screech followed with Sammi Jo and Jake sitting silently on his back.

The merpeople and seahorses of Edenlandia were all crammed into the large cave. The Royal Family, Cody, Cooper and Margo, were sitting on large rocks shaped like chairs at the rear of the cave. Kirstin swam up to join them in her 'chair' as a hush descended upon the crowd.

Cody raised his hand in a motion for everyone to pay attention as he began to speak.

"We have called this town meeting in an effort to notify everyone of impending doom. We waited for Screech and our young human friends to arrive so they could also hear our story. It would not be fair for them to be unaware of the things that may be happening to our village and our land."

The crowd began to murmur amongst themselves as Kirstin arose to begin the story that had been handed down over generations.

4

Legends of the Past

"As you all know; the dragonfly fish have always been our guardians. This tradition began hundreds and hundreds of years ago when our ancestors made an alliance with them. They are small and fast and seem to be everywhere keeping an eye on things. In times of peace, they coexist with us very gracefully. Flitting through our lives in a quiet and graceful manner. We barely even notice that they are there. When they sense danger, they alert us with frantic actions that warn us to hide or take care. However, this time, they are gathering in large numbers around the perimeter of our land. I don't even know where they are all coming from, but their numbers have increased dramatically, and we don't know why."

The crowd began to whisper and shake their heads as if to agree that they, too, had no explanation for the large numbers of dragonfly fish and cuttlefish that had been showing up lately.

"The only time this has ever happened, to our knowledge, was many generations ago. My great-great-great grandfather was the king at that time and the story has been passed down over the generations. The story is one of the uprising of the giant cuttlefish."

"Wait!" shouted Dafne, the littlest mermaid. "The cuttlefish aren't bad they just swim quietly along the bottom of the ocean and never bother us."

"That is true," answered Cody as he stood up to join Kirstin, "But have you noticed that they are camouflaging themselves more now than they used to? They used to allow us to see them freely, but it is almost as if they too are being extra cautious."

"Part of the legend states that the small cuttlefish became very anxious during this time. They walked on their front arms very close to the ocean floor and were clearly trying to blend into the sand where no one could see them," interrupted Cooper, anxious to be a part of the story.

"Because they know us so well, they have not often felt the need to hide. They also know that there are no predators that come close to our land, so feel very safe here. Apparently, they are no longer feeling safe and we don't know why," he continued.

"As you know, we live very near one of the deepest ocean trenches in the world. Although not as deep as the Mariana Trench in the Pacific Ocean, ours is pretty deep. We don't go there because of the mysterious creatures that live below and, according to the legend, there are giant cuttlefish that live in those ocean depths. Only once in history have they come out from the trench and that is the time we are speaking of now."

Kirstin picked up the story again at this point.

"There was once an evil sea dragon that lived amongst us. It loved to scare our children, threaten the seahorses and wreak havoc amongst the village. It became irate that we were always warned of his impending arrival by the dragonfly fish and tried everything it could to trick them into thinking he was good and kind. Now this evil sea dragon, Drakon was his name, began to get an idea. He knew that we trusted the cuttlefish and the dragonfly fish and began to plot how he could turn the cuttlefish against us. He knew the dragonfly fish would never comply, so began his evil plotting against the cuttlefish by treating them nicely and getting them to trust him. This went completely against the nature of the cuttlefish, but over time, he was able to claim a small group of the cuttlefish as his friends and turn them against the other cuttlefish and dragonfly fish."

"But why would they do that?" screamed Violet, one of the smaller merchildren. "Didn't they know he was bad?"

"Yes, they did, but he had convinced them he was to be trusted and they didn't pay attention to the actions of the past, or of the creeds they had grown up with to steer clear of evil. That is why you are scolded when you attempt to break our creeds and laws that we have built our land on and have sustained us for generations. When you steer away from our heritage and our laws, bad things begin to happen," explained Kirstin.

The seahorses had remained silent up to now, but Natasha broke in at this point, as well.

"Yes, youngsters, we too have these same creeds and laws. We do not allow them to be broken and those that do are punished. We have these laws and creeds to keep our communities and our world safe. When we move away from the ideals that have kept us unified for centuries, we risk everything we have come to know and love. Drakon was imposing his wishes on the cuttlefish, and rather than sticking to their history and the heritage their community was built on, they began to change into something he wanted them to be."

The cuttlefish that succumbed to Drakon were soon under his spell.. He began to feed them powerful plants from the depths of the trench. These plants began to transform them and they began to grow larger and larger. They still retained their abilities to blend into their surroundings, but because they were becoming so large, they were also becoming more dangerous. As they became more dependent on Drakon and his powerful plants, they began to turn on the creatures and friends in the village and young merpeople and seahorses began to disappear ...

A war was soon waged against Drakon and his army of large cuttlefish. All the creatures of the deep banded together to fight Drakon. The sharks, octopi, squid, whales, etc... All joined arms to send Drakon and his evil minions back to the depths of the trench. The battle was long and hard, but eventually Drakon was forced to return to his trench, along with his evil cuttlefish."

"They have not been seen again," whispered Kirstin solemnly.

"We are afraid that they are making a reappearance," stated Natacha. "And, if so, we need to be prepared to battle again. Everyone needs to be super diligent and report anything strange or unusual you may see, especially if you see areas of land and water that may seem to be questionable. Even though the cuttlefish can blend in with their surroundings, the area where they are "hiding" will not look exactly the same as the area around them."

Everyone began to murmur nervously amongst themselves as the meeting broke up and everyone began to return cautiously back to their homes and duties for the day.

Kirstin and Cody excused themselves and swam up to Screech. They asked him to keep a close eye out for anything unusual and suggested that, perhaps, Sammi Jo and Jake may want to stay away for a while in case there really was something dangerous out there.

"No way!" exclaimed Sammi Jo. "You are our people too and we are here to help in any way that we can possibly can!"

"We will be back tomorrow," announced Jake solemnly, "and will help you all track down this Drakon and his evil cuttlefish. We will do all we can to make this place safe again!"

Kirstin gave them both a big hug to show how much she appreciated what they were willing to do for the people of Edenlandia. Screech slid silently away with Sammi Jo and Jake keeping a very close eye on their surroundings as they ascended quickly to the surface.

5

Strange New Friends

Sammi Jo and Jake left early the next morning after making Mr. and Mrs. Meriwether promise to make the calls to the adoption agency and to tell them everything just as soon as they returned. Although they didn't really want to miss out on the phone call, they knew that the people of Edenlandia were in distress and wanted to get there as soon as possible to see if they could help.

Screech was already at their beach cove anxiously waiting for them and they quickly donned their masks and translators and swam out to jump on Screeches back. They did not have much time for chit chat this morning and Screech dove quickly under the water, after throwing them a very worried glance over his shoulder and reminding them to keep a close eye on their surroundings.

Cody and Cooper and several others were awaiting them as they arrived. They all appeared very solemn and scared and were carrying long, dangerous looking swords.

"Good morning," greeted Cody.

"What's going on?" questioned Sammi Jo. "I didn't know you guys had weapons!"

"Obviously, these weapons are not something we choose to bring out often, but we are going on a quest to the trench to see what we can find and feel that we need some protection. The weapons are kept in a large locked cave and are only brought out in times of dire need."

"Crazy...," breathed Jake with wide eyes. "What do you think you will find at the trench? Can we go?"

"Yes, you can go, but we need you to stay with Screech. We don't know what we are going to find, but we do have some 'friends' that stay near the trench and they will let us know if they have noticed anything odd going on lately."

"Friends?" asked Sammi Jo curiously, "What kind of friends are they?"

"You'll see," said Cody, "You will be very surprised, I can guarantee that!"

At that, he turned around and swam away with Cooper and the others following him closely.

Jake and Sammi Jo shrugged their shoulders and urged Screech to follow quickly.

They swam deeper and deeper into the ocean and it became darker and darker. Sammi Jo began to feel a little scared and was getting pretty cold when they finally glided to a stop. The water around them was very dark and still and they could barely see anything!

"I can't see!" whispered Sammi Jo quietly as she anxiously peered around her, opening her eyes as wide as they would go.

"Hold on," said Screech, "things will brighten up soon."

"What do you mean...?" Sammi Jo began, as her voice trailed off in awe.

A glow was beginning to appear in front of them as hundreds of little fish began to appear over the edge of the trench. They didn't even know that they were near the trench as they had been unable to see before. But, now, in the glow of fish, they could see the enormous drop off that appeared before them.

"What are they?" whispered Jake.

"They are called lanternfish," replied Screech. "We rarely see them, but they seem to always know when we are near and come out of the trench to help us out."

Some of the fish were really tiny while others seemed to be about a foot long. They formed a huge circle around the mermen, Sammi Jo, Jake, and Screech, while their glowing scales provided enough light for everyone to finally see where they were.

As Sammi Jo's eyes adjusted to the dim light, she gasped and stared at what could only be described as a "ghost ship."

"Do you see that?" she finally managed to splutter out.

In front of them was a large ship. Its sails were tattered and torn and the wood was decaying. There was also a tattered pirate flag hanging mournfully off the broken mast. Fish of all sorts were swimming about and darting in and out of the broken sections of wood. It was like something straight out of a movie!

As they continued to gape at the ship, they began to see ghostly figures emerging from the wreckage. The images appeared to be parrots dressed in pirate clothing!

"What the ...", muttered Jake under his breath.

Cody and Cooper came rushing up at this point to explain.

"These are the 'friends' I was telling you about," stated Cody.

"The ship was wrecked here in the late 1800's on a pirating mission. The parrots you see were captives of the pirates and have remained with the ship all this time. We have become good friends and because they stick close to the ship, they are always happy to let us know if there is anything unusual going on near or around the trench."

The "parrots" began to "fly" towards the group as Sammi Jo cowered behind Screech. She had seen lots of strange things since their ocean adventures began, but this was definitely not something she had been prepared to see!

Although they were transparent, they looked pretty much like normal parrots (with exception of wearing pirate stuff). They were squawking and screeching and shoving as they floated toward Sammi Jo and Jake.

"Hello," whispered one of the parrot ghosts in a strange squawky whisper. "It has been a very long time since we have seen humans! We are very pleased to make your acquaintance!"

Sammi Jo's mouth opened and closed, but she could not seem to utter a word.

A second parrot ghost swam up close to Sammi Jo and began to introduce the group.

"My name is Minnie," she stated, "and the others are Petey, Percy, and Nellie. You don't need to be afraid of us. We are not actually pirates! We belonged to the dastardly pirates that went down with this ship many years ago. We have stayed with our ship because of the great friends from Edenlandia that made us feel so welcome."

"Well ... it is very nice to meet you ..." gasped Sammi Jo as she finally got her mouth to work again.

She attempted to shake hands, but that didn't work too well as they were ... well ... ghosts ... and parrots!

"We know that this is another new thing for you to have to grasp right now," stated Cody, "but we need to get down to business. We don't know what is going on and we need to talk to the parrots about what they may have seen."

"Of course," sputtered Jake. "We understand!"

The "parrots" gathered around and began to relay the events that had been happening lately.

6

Drakon Lives!

Petey is the one who seemed to be the storyteller as he began telling of the strange events that had been going on over the past few weeks.

Their squeaky parrot voices were a little difficult to understand, but the story went something like this …

"Well, things were pretty normal around here until a couple of weeks ago. We began to see the water shimmering where it shouldn't be and many of our fish friends seem to be staying away. We weren't sure of what was happening until Drakon appeared."

"You mean the Drakon from the legends?" interrupted Sammi Jo.

"Yes, that's the one," answered Petey. "But that is not all, there was someone else with Drakon!"

"Who?" broke in Cody.

Percy spoke up at this point.

"Do you remember the merman you told us about a long time ago? The one who decided not to stay with you all after the gathering? The one who decided to follow a different path?"

"Of course," said Cooper, "that was Tekoah. No one has seen him in years and we didn't know where he had gone."

"Well," continued Percy, "Apparently he has decided to make the trench his home and side with Drakon and his evil gang of sea dragons!"

"What?!" shouted Cody, "That is not possible! Tekoah was a good merman! Why would he do that?"

"Keep in mind," reminded Cooper, "that he did decide to leave us and all he had ever known.

Perhaps there was more going on in his head than we knew about."

Everyone began to talk at the same time. Trying to figure out why Tekoah had joined up with Drakon, what it could mean, why it had happened... There was so much confusion that finally, the smallest ghost parrot, Nellie, put up her wing and slapped it angrily and silently in water!

"Do you want to hear the story, or do you just want to try and make up the story yourself?"

Everyone apologized for interrupting and Petey continued the story.

Petey began talking again. "As I said the water was shimmery where it shouldn't have been and when Percy and I went over to investigate, a sea dragon appeared in place of the shimmers."

"Yes," interrupted Minnie. "Nellie and I were watching from the ship when the dragon appeared out of nowhere. Apparently, they have learned how to camouflage themselves and the only way of knowing is by the shimmery water, if you look close enough."

"That sounds like the story of the cuttlefish that Kirstin was telling us about," spoke up Sammi Jo. "Except that no one ever mentioned that the dragons could camouflage themselves, too"

"It gets even more strange, though," said Petey. "As soon as the dragon discovered that it had uncovered itself and had been discovered, it transformed into a very large cuttlefish and scurried off across the ocean floor!"

Everyone began talking at once. No one had ever heard of such a thing. No wonder all of the cuttlefish had been acting so strangely and the dragonfly fish had been protective. From the way it sounded, the people of Edenlandia would have no clue if there were dragons (or cuttlefish) stalking their community as they had learned to disguise themselves so well.

It seemed as though the magic weeds that Drakon had been feeding the cuttlefish years ago had not only made them grow, but somehow, had given them the ability to transform into sea dragons!

Cody, spoke up again, at that point, to address Petey.

"You said that Tekoah was with Drakon. When and how did you happen to see that?"

"The cuttlefish that ran away from me disappeared over the edge of the trench, so we can only guess that it went to tell Drakon that it had been discovered," replied Petey.

"And then came Drakon ..." Nellie began.

"Shush!" said Petey, "I'm telling the story! So, as Nellie said, then came Drakon, in all his glory, up over the side of the trench, and right beside him was a mean looking merman sitting atop an equally mean looking seahorse. Of course, we didn't know it was Tekoah at that time – we only knew it was a pretty "mean" looking merman!"

"Drakon glided right over to us and demanded to know what we were doing here by his trench. I told him we had been here for over a century and that we couldn't hardly move from this spot ... he seemed very surprised that he had never noticed us before, but was probably too busy planning his revenge..."

"Wait!" called out Cody, "What revenge? What do you mean by planning his revenge? What have we ever done to Drakon?"

"Well, you all may not have been around during the great war when he was banished from your kingdom, but dragons live very long lives and he still remembers the war and the way all the ocean creatures raged against him. He has not been happy living in the trench all these years and has had a long, long time to get and stay angry. He has been preparing the cuttlefish to help him in battle, along with the other few dragons he has gathered up over the years."

"But what about Tekoah," asked Cooper, "What did he have to say?"

Minnie spoke up at this point saying, "Tekoah mostly sat there on his horse Saqua. He made us very uncomfortable since we are not used to being around a merman that sides with the evil things in life. Eventually, he spoke up to say that he had been helping Drakon to learn the ways of his people so that the dragons would have a better chance."

"Of course, neither of them had any idea, that we are friends with you," said Nellie with a big smile, "so, they thought their secrets were safe!"

"Well, that is a relief," said Sammi Jo, "but, what did Tekoah or Saqua have to say about why they turned against Edenlandia? It just seems odd..."

"It has been a long time since I have seen Tekoah," said Cody, "But he was never a very happy child or teenager. He seemed to feel he was always being picked on. None of the rest of us felt that way, but he began to withdraw more and more as we approached the date of the Gathering, those many years ago. His horse, Saqua, had been a beautiful and kind horse, but the more Tekoah withdrew, the more Saqua withdrew, until they both just kept to themselves most of the time."

"After the Gathering when they decided to part ways with our kingdom, they both swam away, and no one has ever heard of them since. It absolutely broke our hearts, and especially the hearts of his parents..."

"That is so sad," said Sammi Jo, "Maybe one day we will know the reason, but first I guess we should get back to Edenlandia and start to make a plan."

"Great idea!" spoke up Cooper. "Let's go!"

The ghost parrots promised to keep them updated on anything new and floated slowly back to their ship as Sammi Jo, Screech, Jake, and the others, began to swim back to Edenlandia.

"You two have sure been quiet," said Sammi Jo questioningly to Jake and Screech. "What is going on in your heads?"

"Too surprised to speak," said Screech. "My family used to be friends with Drakon and his family a long time ago. It's perplexing that he would turn out this way and that he seems to be so bent on revenge for something we could not even control. It will be interesting to be able to talk to him when and if the time comes."

"Yeah," said Jake, "Yeah..."

"Well, I gotta tell you, that I am pretty surprised also! I am astonished at the fact that we met parrots, under the sea! Parrots that are ghosts and can talk just like humans," stated Sammi Jo emphatically.

Screech just winked at her and swam on, while Jake continued to muse in a very thoughtful silence.

7

Word Travels Fast!

By the time Sammi Jo and the others had returned to Edenlandia, the place with abuzz with the news!

"How does everyone know already?" asked Sammi Jo is a very perplexed voice. "We just got here!"

"Ah...," replied Screech with a smile. "The ocean has a vast **Social Media** network!"

"What do you mean? Like Facebook, or what?" demanded Jake! "I'm sure that you don't have underwater computers... Do you?

"No," laughed Screech and Cody at the same time. "Our version is far simpler than yours. We are constantly surrounded by sea life. Small and large, from sea anemones to snails to amoebas – anyone or anything, could have overheard our conversation with the parrots – and passed it on to the next, and then to the next, etc... It doesn't take long for word to travel down here with our VAST network of sea life."

"Oh, haha!" said Sammi Jo, "You were making FUN of our social media network, weren't you? I gotta admit – yours seems to work every bit as well! And... everyone actually has to talk with each other!"

They quickly made their way to the meeting cave to find Kirstin surrounded by stone tablets of all shapes and sizes. They were covered in pictures and writing and littered the entire floor of the cave. She barely looked up as they entered; she was so intent on her task.

"What's going on?" asked Cody.

"I feel that we must be missing something," Kirstin replied. "What happened so long ago to make Drakon and his gang so angry?"

"We can help!" piped up Sammi Jo. "Where should we start?"

"I have everything laid out according to years. I am working on the first section of tablets from the first year that we begin to keep records. You and Jake can start on the next group, and then Cody and the boys can start on the next group. That should make this go a lot faster. Just keep an eye out about anything referring to dragons."

Each group moved to their section and Screech stuck with Kirstin to help her. Everyone was mostly quiet, except for the occasional "What?" or "Really?" but mostly there was silence, until...

"Eureka!" shouted Jake.

Everyone's heads popped up to stare as he waved a tablet around his head in excitement!

"I found it! I really found it!"

All the others came rushing over to see what he had found.

Jake was so excited, he could barely speak and his face had turned bright red with embarrassment now that all the attention was on him.

"Well, spill it!" coaxed Sammi Jo gently. "What have you found?"

"It looks like something happened long before the war that you guys were talking about," he said to Kirstin. "And long before your dad was even king," he said to Cody.

"From what I can see here, the people of Edenlandia were friends with the dragons at one time, they worked together, played together and the dragons actually helped to guard the kingdom. They worked closely with the dragonfly fish and the cuttlefish to ensure that no harm would come to the land. In fact, they had their own clan of dragons and Drakon was their leader. Over time, many of the dragons had died out, much like Screeches kind, but those that were left had committed themselves to protecting Edenlandia."

"Drakon had two brothers by the names of Zurka and Lyzer and a sister named Kyree. Because there were no other dragons, that they knew of, they knew that their family and their breed was dying out! Knowing that there would be no more dragons caused Kyree a lot of grief as she so wanted to be a mom."

"She decided to leave Edenlandia to see if she could find another pod of dragons somewhere in the vast ocean. It was her plan to unite them so they could form a new community and keep their kind and their breed alive and thriving."

Jake paused to take a break, and the others began to look over the tablets to see what happened then.

"Oh look!" cried Sammi Jo. "It looks like she found some others!"

"Yes, I believe so," said Jake. "But, it doesn't look like it was the best find... "

* 59 *

Cooper had taken the tablet by this time and was reading silently with a frown between his brows. When he finally looked up, it was to give them a look of dismay.

"It says here that Kyree returned to Edenlandia after being gone for many months. Drakon and his brothers were ecstatic to see her again as they had been very worried."

"They were equally excited to see that she had actually found some other sea dragons. It sounded as if they had been part of the original clan that had been lost years before."

"Kyree introduced them as Lurko and Maximus and it looked as if perhaps she and Maximus had struck up quite a friendship during their travels since they seemed to stick pretty close to each other."

Sammi Jo was quite excited by all of this as it looked as if the dragon clan might be rebuilt after all, but...

"So, what happened then? It sounds as if everything is working out great!"

Jake took the tablet back and was quiet for several minutes before he spoke up again.

"Well, from what this says, Lurko and Maximus had actually been banished from the clan many years before as they both seemed to have a mean streak. Although it was very hard on the dragon clan and the people of Edenlandia, they had learned that Lurko and Maximus were not to be trusted and they had been told to leave and never return!"

"Except that Kyree didn't know that!" said Sammi Jo in dismay. "She brought them back without even knowing that they were not nice."

"Yep, that's what it looks like," said Jake.

Kirstin took the tablet from Jake at that point and began to quickly skim what was left of the story.

"Lurko and Maximus began to raid the town, they burned buildings, kidnapped children, and wreaked havoc on the kingdom of Edenlandia. Once again, they were asked to leave, but this time, they refused."

"The creatures of the sea bound together to rid our kingdom of these two evil sea dragons. During the battle, Kyree disappeared and Drakon's two brothers were killed."

"No wonder he is so angry," said Sammi Jo sadly. "He lost his whole family... "

"By the end of the battle," continued Kirstin, "Everything and everyone that Drakon had loved was lost. He retreated to the trench and was never seen again until recent history when he came back and began to turn the cuttlefish against us."

"For some reason, he seems to blame Edenlandia for the loss of his family, even though it was actually the other two dragons that caused it. There must be some way to get through to him," mused Jake.

"I'm not sure he is able to listen," said Cody. "He has turned Tekoah and many of the cuttlefish against us. He is planning a battle and we may just have to fight to save our land..."

8

Is It Really Happening?

Sammi Jo and Jake were both very subdued as they arrived back at the cottage, but that soon changed as Sammi Jo's parents began talking excitedly about the news they had to share!

"It is an amazing thing that today is the day you chose to talk with your mom about wanting siblings!" her dad began.

"Why? What happened?" Sammi Jo broke in excitedly.

"I got a phone call from the adoption agency while I was in town today and they have two kids that they think will be a perfect match for us!"

"No way! Seriously?" breathed Sammi Jo. "This is happening so fast! I guess THIS is going to be the BEST day ever!"

"Hold on," laughed her dad. "I didn't say they were coming today! These two kids have had it pretty rough and have lived in several different foster homes together. They have only had each other for a very long time and have become very close. They are not biologically related, but have been together for so long, that they absolutely must both go to the same home."

"That is so sad," replied Sammi Jo. "I hope that we are able to give them the home they seem to need so bad," and then brightened up as she stated, "Maybe they could come and visit and if they like us, they could stay! Wouldn't that be cool?"

"Yes, it would," replied her mom. "But, what if they don't? Then how will you feel?"

"Oh, they will!" exclaimed Sammi Jo vehemently. "We have plenty of love for everyone. We have a cottage on the beach, we have an awesome school to go to, and we get to go on great vacations. I could teach them how to HAVE THE BEST DAY EVER! They will just have to give us a chance, especially when I tell them about the great adventures we can have together and all about SCR...., well, all about the

sea and the amazing creatures it holds, and teach them
how to swim, if they don't already know, and..." she
trailed off. "Well, and so much other stuff! Can we ask
them for a visit, please... "

"Well, with all of that, how could they refuse?"
chuckled her dad. "I will call the agency back in the
morning and see what we can work out. You haven't
even asked yet if they are boys or girls."

"I don't actually care," said Sammi Jo. "It would be
great if one was a girl, so she could room with Kara and
I once we go back to school, but ... I am fine either
way!"

"Lucky you then," replied her mom. "There is a boy
and a girl! The boy is ten and the girl is eight, so she
would actually get to be in classes with you as well as
staying with you and Kara in the dorm. The boy is
pretty used to taking care of the girl, so he may not
want to be separated ... but perhaps he would really
like to hang out with some boys his age for once."

"Do you know their names?"

"No, they wouldn't tell me their names until we
make all the arrangements and talked with you about
it," her dad replied. "But, perhaps we will know after

the phone call tomorrow. We'll talk it about it more then." And then, turning to Jake, "You're pretty quiet, what do you think about all of this?"

"I think it is amazing," he sighed. "I know that Sammi Jo will be the best sister ever and they won't be able to resist being a part of your family. I hope they get to come soon so that I can meet them before it is time for me to head home."

"We do too!" said Sammi Jo's mom with eyes that were just slightly too bright (as if she were trying to hold back tears). "We do too... it will be a dream come true for all of us!"

"All right everyone! Let's get washed up for dinner and then maybe we could have a bonfire to help celebrate all of our new possibilities! We haven't done that for a while and I think it would be a perfect way to cap off the what could possibly be a perfect day!"

"You mean ... The best day EVER!" screamed Sammi Jo with delight!

Everyone scattered to get cleaned up for dinner and Mr. Meriwether disappeared to quickly gather up some driftwood for a bonfire before it got too dark to see. As he was gathering the wood, he could have sworn something was watching him from the sea, but everyone time he turned around, nothing was there. Just a big, loud "splash." He simply shook his head and wandered back up to the house for dinner. He knew he would not tell Sammi Jo about it or he would get her head spinning again with thoughts of what may be out there, as she had done their very first night at the cottage.

9

Battle Plans and More ...

The battle plans began in earnest after Sammi Jo and Jake arrived the next day!

No one had any idea where to start as none of them had ever been involved in something so dangerous. They only knew that Drakon was planning an attack and they had to be ready.

"Let's send out scouts to the trench to see if they can see or hear something that will help us prepare," said Jake.

"Let's also send out scouts to start gathering other ocean creatures to help us," Sammi Jo piped up.

They found the tablets that had a map of their area and the surrounding oceans. It showed where the trench was and the rocks and outcroppings surrounding the trench.

"This is a great place to start," said Kirstin, "We can use this to help us figure out where we can hide and prepare for Drakon and Tekoah as they come over the trench!"

"Can we write on this tablet?" asked Sammi Jo.

Some of the others were gathering up flat stones to use for new tablets, while others were finding small sharp shells to "write" with. Being as they were under the water, traditional paper and pencils would not work very well.

They began to make lists on one of the tablets:

1.   Send scouts to the trench.

2.   Make sure the ghost parrots knew to keep them updated if they heard or saw anything new.

3.   Send scouts out to begin to gather any and all of the oceans creatures that would be willing to help.

4. Search all of the nearby caves to find any of the ancient weapons that may be stored.

"Hey!" shouted Sammi Jo. "Since the ghost parrots live on an old pirate ship, I wonder if there happens to be cannon on board?"

5. Ask parrots about a cannon and if anyone can figure out how to make it work under water.

"You know," said Cooper, "Cody has always been pretty good at figuring out how to make stuff work. Maybe he can figure out how to make a cannon work underwater... if they have one."

6. Have Cody figure out how to make the cannon work (if there is one).

"What else can we do to prepare?" asked Sammi Jo. "I think this is super hard 'cuz I don't think anyone here has ever needed to do something like this before... Can we update the map to make any changes that have happened since the original map was created?"

    7. Update map.

The children all furrowed their brows as they concentrated on what else they should do to prepare. It would be nice if King Richard would magically make an appearance, as he had been through this before and would probably know what to do ... or even Queen Alicia and King William – they had never been through a battle, but would have great ideas just because they were used to running a kingdom.

    8. Send someone to Westlandia to see if we
       could get some help!

Kirstin began to hand out assignments to everyone and they all agreed to meet back in the cave the next morning to see what progress had been made.

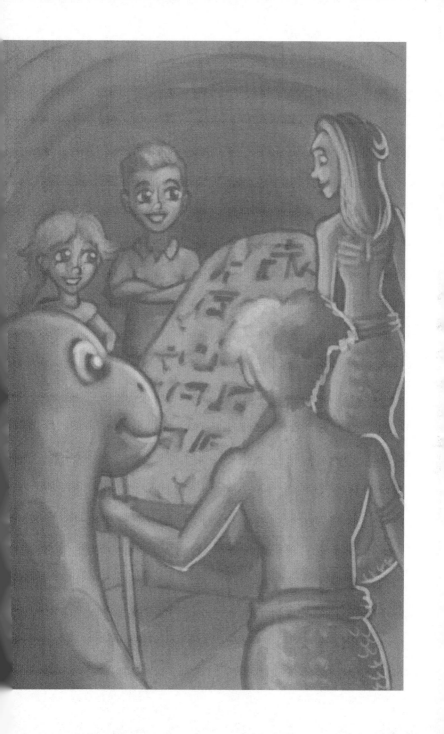

Cody was assigned to search for ancient weapons and then instruct everyone how to use them ... if he found any.

The crowd broke up as they all started to gather up others to help them with their tasks. Sammi Jo and Jake didn't really have any tasks as they couldn't swim fast enough to reach everyone in the ocean, so Screech took them home, so he could get started on his duties. He was going to talk to his parents and see if they could help. They are HUGE – so they should be able to do something. AND they actually knew Drakon as they were both involved in the first battle, so... well, it couldn't hurt...

It was still pretty early when Screech dropped off Sammi Jo and Jake at the beach, so they settled themselves under the tree to discuss everything that was going on. They were astonished at all they learned and couldn't even imagine that there could be such evil in a place that they had learned to love so much!

Jake was staring at the sea thinking about what they could do to help when he noticed something bobbing on the surface a little bit beyond the rock.

"Hey Sammi Jo! Do you see what I see?"

Sammi Jo lifted her hand up to shield her eyes from the glare as she stared and stared...

"I don't see anything," she said. "What do you think you saw?"

"I'm not sure," Jake said slowly. "It was as if something had waved at me from the surface of the water."

"That's just like when I first met Screech," stated Sammi Jo, "I kept thinking I was seeing things, and then he finally revealed himself! I wonder if this will be the same way..."

They both walked down to the water's edge to see if they could get a closer look. They were so busy staring into the ocean that they both jumped as they heard a voice say ...

"Hello!"

Right in front of them was a sea turtle! He had a huge grin on his face as he held out his flipper to shake their hands.

"My name is Arkeo!" he announced loudly. "You must be Jake and Sammi Jo!"

"How do you know that?" questioned Sammi Jo.

"Oh, everyone has heard about the two of you! I have come all the way from North Carolina to meet you two! There is a large population of us along the North Carolina coast and I have been sent to check you both out!"

"What kind of sea turtle are you?" asked Sammi Jo.

"I am a leatherback," Arkeo stated proudly. There are actually many of us up in this part of the country. The water here is much colder, but because we can generate our own heat, we can hang out in the colder waters of the East coast."

"Why did you decide to come visit us? Have you heard of the troubles in Edenlandia?" queried Jake.

"No...," stated Arkeo curiously. "We just wanted to see what it would be like to talk with humans. What are you talking about?"

Sammi Jo began to relate the stories of Drakon and his plan to take over Edenlandia. She told him all about the history of Drakon and his family of sea dragons, the cuttlefish and the dragonfly fish and ended up telling about how one of the "wayward" mermen, Tekoah, was helping him out and how the whole kingdom was gathering up sea creatures to help defend the kingdom against them.

"That is quite the story," said Arkeo. "What can we do to help?"

"The more creatures we have to defend the kingdom, the better," Stated Jake solemnly. "Do you think you could gather up your numbers and have them meet us outside of Edenlandia tomorrow?"

"Absolutely! We would be pleased to help! I am very young, but some of our elders are huge and . weigh a whole lot. With our tough shells, we should be able to defend ourselves and Edenlandia with ease!"

"I will see you tomorrow with as many turtles as I can gather together by then. We will pass the word so that more can come from further distances."

With that, he lifted a flipper to wave goodbye and disappeared into the water.

"Oh my gosh!" exclaimed Sammi Jo. "That was so cool! We get to check something off the list that we didn't even know was there!"

Feeling very pleased with themselves and the surprise they would be able to present to the kingdom of Edenlandia, they turned and started towards home, so deep in thought that they didn't even notice an unfamiliar car parked at the house ...

10

Whose Car is That?

"**H**ey, look!" exclaimed Sammi Jo as they approached the house. "Whose car is that?"

"Dunno," mumbled Jake, as he glanced toward the driveway.

He was way too distracted by his thoughts of the troubles in Edenlandia to be paying much attention.

"Who's here?" hollered Sammi Jo excitedly as she burst through the kitchen door.

"Hush, Sammi Jo!" scolded her mom. "Mrs. Gilmore is from the adoption agency in town, and she is here to interview our family to see if we may be a good fit for the children she has in mind to join our family."

"I'm very sorry for being rude," said Sammi Jo. "It is so nice to meet you! This is Jake, my cousin." She added, pointing in Jake's direction.

"It is no problem," answered Mrs. Gilmore, with a smile. "It is so nice to see kids that are happy and excited to come home."

"Now that Sammi Jo and Jake are here, I guess we can get started," said Mr. Meriwether nervously. "Where should we start?"

"There is nothing to be nervous about," laughed Mrs. Gilmore. "I am only here to get to know you better and to make sure that you all are ready to grow your family. It is a huge commitment and some people are not really prepared to add additional children to their household."

"Oh!" exclaimed Sammi Jo, "we are SO ready to have additional children in our home! That is why Jake is here, so I would have someone to hang out with at the beach all summer."

"Well, we also have Scree...," started Jake and then stopped suddenly, turning bright red as he realized what he was about to say.

"What was that?" asked Mrs. Gilmore curiously. "Do you have another friend on the beach that you play with?"

"It's only Screech," said Sammi Jo quickly. "He meets us at the beach every day and we play and make up stories and imagine what life under the sea might be like."

"Will you tell me about some of the adventures you have made up?" asked Mrs. Gilmore.

"Of course! We have had many exciting adventures with merpeople and seahorses and underwater adventures! Right now, we are planning on a big battle to help defend the kingdom. There is an evil sea dragon who is threatening the people of Edenlandia and all the creatures of the sea are banding together to help!"

"My, my," said Mrs. Gilmore with a smile on her face. "You certainly do have a vivid imagination!"

"Yes, she does," agreed Mr. Meriwether. "We feel fairly certain that she will grow up to be a writer just like her mom and dad!"

They all laughed about that and Jake and Sammi Jo exchanged "secret" glances. They knew that no one would ever think that their stories were true, so there wasn't any harm in talking about it!

Sammi Jo's mom went to the kitchen to get some drinks and snacks and Mrs. Gilmore turned a smiling face to Sammi Jo.

"What do you think will be the most exciting part about having some siblings?"

"I have the greatest life!" exclaimed Sammi Jo. "The only thing that we are missing is other children! I have a great family and great friends, but there are definitely times that it gets really lonely and I would love to have siblings to share things with!"

"You don't think that it would be hard to get to used to having to share your parents love, or maybe get jealous because you are not getting ALL the attention?" asked Mrs. Gilmore.

"Oh NO!" exclaimed Sammi Jo vehemently. "I have wanted brothers or sisters my whole life! I haven't been able to think about anything else ever since Mom and I first talked about this!"

"She is even jealous of me having a brother," added Jake solemnly. "I told her she could have mine." He finished with a big grin.

"Oh, I doubt you would really like that!" laughed Mrs. Gilmore with a grin.

Mr. and Mrs. Meriwether came back into the room with some drinks and snacks to share while Mrs. Gilmore began to tell them about the children.

"These children are not related, but have spent many years in foster care together and we all feel it would be best if they could to a family together. They are all they family that they remember..."

"Of course!" exclaimed Mr. and Mrs. Meriwether together. "We would love to take both children!"

"The boy is ten years old and his name is Jase, the girl is eight, same as you Sammi Jo, and her name is Riley. They were put into foster care at the same time several years ago and Jase immediately seemed to take Riley under his wing. They are very, very close and would be lost without each other. Since Jase has always been the "dad" to Riley, he may need to adjust to having someone else in charge."

"We will all help," Sammi Jo spoke up.

"And...," she began, "There is one more small detail to talk about."

"What's that?" asked Mr. Meriwether.

"Well... they have a dog ..."

"Oh my gosh! A dog! That would be AWESOME!" cried Sammi Jo.

Her parents looked at each questioningly and then smiled and shrugged their shoulders.

"What kind of a dog?"

"He is a white boxer named Jack. Very friendly and very well behaved. He is the one item that Jase has left from his biological family. They had recently gotten him when Jase had to be placed in foster care and where ever Jase goes, Jack goes."

Everyone assured Mrs. Gilmore that they would work it out and that it might be fun to have a dog around for a change.

She finally rose to leave assuring them that she would get back with them in a few to get everything finalized and arrange to have the kids come and meet the Meriwether family.

Everyone thanked her and told her how excited they were for this new adventure as they walked her to her car and watched her drive away.

They all began to talk excitedly about the visit and all the possibilities and when it was going to happen and IF it was going to happen and what it would be like to have a dog around.

Mr. Meriwether promised that he would call the boarding school and see if they would be willing to take two more children and to possibly have a school "mascot." There would be no way they could have a dog if the school was not willing to accept the dog along with the two new children.

It was an exciting dinner and evening and they began to dream and imagine and, of course, to BELIEVE that it truly would!

"Oh my gosh," breathed Sammi Jo as she headed to bed. "This has definitely been the BEST DAY EVER!"

I wonder if I should write Kara tonight. But, she hadn't heard back from Kara in several days, so figured that they must be busy and would just write her tomorrow...

11

So Many Creatures!

Sammi Jo and Jake had been sitting on the beach for over half an hour waiting for Screech to show up.

"This is so odd..." murmured Sammi Jo. "Screech is never late, and he is usually waiting for us to show up. I hope nothing has happened."

"It is odd," Jake responded, "But maybe he just got caught up in the plans and forgot to come and get us."

"That would never happen!" exclaimed Sammi Jo.

"Well, things happen..." Jake trailed off as stared at the ocean, his eyes getting wider and wider.

"Look!" he shouted

Sammi Jo turned her eyes toward the sea, raising her hand to shield the sun from her eyes. Her eyes widened, her mouth dropped open and she stood there speechless as she gazed toward the sea.

The water was teeming with sea creatures of every size and shape and leading the group were Screech with a huge grin on his face and their newest friend, Arkeo, the sea turtle. Arkeo had his flipper in the air and was waving wildly at Jake and Sammi Jo.

"See, I told you I had a huge family!" he shouted as he indicated the sea behind him.

There were hundreds of leatherback turtles, in all shapes and sizes! Some appeared to be huge, but it was kind of hard to tell at this distance. He really did have an enormous family!

Apparently, the word had travelled quickly and there seemed to be no end to the numbers and types of sea creatures that were swarming towards the shore. Sammi Jo really hoped that neither of her parents happened to be looking out the windows at this moment because she had no idea how she would be able to explain this to them or anyone else who happened to be seeing this phenomenal event!

There were dolphins and porpoises jumping through the air. Orcas were randomly appearing in

beautiful flashes of black and white. Shark fins sliced the water in huge numbers and sailfish and swordfish sliced the air in huge leaping arcs!

The surface of the water was rippled with hundreds of other fish in all shapes and sizes that had all gathered to offer their assistance to the people of Edenlandia and to help defend them against the evil Drakon and his small band of transforming cuttlefish!

Screech swam up to their normal meeting spot and gestured to them to come and climb on his back.

"Are you sure it is okay," questioned Sammi Jo fearfully. "I mean there are sharks in the water and I'm not really comfortable with swimming with sharks..."

"Everything is fine," answered Screech. "The sharks have no interest in eating you. They are here on a mission to help and would certainly not harm you as you are here for the same reason they are. As you can see, there are many creatures here that would normally be food for the sharks. We are all in agreement that, for our mission, everyone is a friend, and NO ONE is food for anyone else!"

"Okay, if you are sure," replied Sammi Jo doubtfully.

She and Jake waded into the water and swam out to climb on Screeches back. He quickly dove into the sea and they began their journey towards Edenlandia.

The trip was amazing as they had never swum with so many different creatures before! Aja and a large group of Sting Rays showed up to glide silently beside them and a group of dolphins grinned at them as they jumped and swam merrily at their sides.

One of the dolphins, Echo, swam up close to talk with Sammi Jo and Jake.

"Hi guys!" he called out enthusiastically. "I know that you are a little nervous about the sharks, but don't you worry at all. We are here for you. As you know, sharks are a little afraid of dolphins, so we will stay close to make sure you are safe and ward away any sharks who may decide to get a little too close for you."

"Thank you so much!" replied Sammi Jo. "That makes me feel a lot better!"

Echo bobbed his head and quickly swam up to the surface to get a breath of air. Several other dolphins took his place while he was gone, showing that they were taking their jobs very seriously!

The water around them was so full of creatures that they were having a difficult time trying to pick out the new ones as they arrived.

At one point, a huge shadow fell over them as an enormous blue whale dwarfed all the others with his size.

"Wow!" exclaimed Jake laughingly. "Imagine ... we are swimming beside a blue whale! I am beginning to think that I am going to be a marine biologist when I grow up. I would love to know so much more about all of the animals, and I kind of think that I may have a little bit of insight into the ocean that others may not have..."

"I think that would be a pretty good bet!" Sammi Jo replied. "In fact, I think I will join you. We could be the best marine biologist team out there!"

They eventually arrived at Edenlandia with their huge gathering of sea creatures and were met by Kirstin, Cody, and many of the people of Edenlandia.

"This is so cool!" breathed Cody. "How ever did you guys manage to accomplish this over night?"

Arkeo pushed his way to the front of the group, stating proudly that he had been a large part of the gathering everyone together. His huge family had passed the word and here they were!

Kirstin nodded solemnly to the group and raised her had to speak.

"We are so grateful to each and every one of you for working together to help us defend our land! We will never be able to repay you for all you have done and all you are willing to do. Please know that we will do anything in our power to help any of you in the future. You just need to send us word and we will be there for you. Right now, though, we will need to get organized and decide how we are going to approach this with so many of you. Arkeo, can you please get everyone organized into groups so that we can decide who will do what?"

"You bet!" he exclaimed with delight. "And immediately swam off to begin dividing everyone into groups.

The others swam through the gates to Edenlandia to meet in the cave while they put together their strategy and being to check items off their list that they had prepared yesterday.

1.   Send scouts to the trench – **The scouts had returned from the trench to report that it appeared that Drakon had a lot more transforming cuttlefish than they had originally planned and that apparently, they had been taught how to breathe fire while they were in their dragon form.**

2.   Make sure the ghost parrots knew to keep them updated if they heard or saw anything new. **The ghost parrots were completely on board and were sending fish back to Edenlandia to make hourly reports.**

3.   Send scouts out to begin to gather all the oceans creatures that would be willing to help. **This had, obviously, been accomplished!**

4.   Search all the nearby caves to find any of the ancient weapons that may be stored. **Cooper reported that he had found a huge stash of rusty old swords and had put a group together to clean them up and get them ready.**

5.   Ask ghost parrots about a cannon and if anyone can figure out how to make it work under water. **There was a cannon on the ship with plenty of cannon balls – so they are good on that one.**

6.   Have Cody figure out how to make the cannon work (if there is one). **Cody had come up with a plan, too technical to tell everyone about, but he was sure he would be able to get the cannon to work, if it became necessary.**

7.   Update map. **Kirstin, Margo, and several of the others, had swum to the boundaries of Edenlandia and all the way to the trench and had updated the map with areas to hide and cover.**

8.   Send someone to Westlandia to see if we could get some help! **The scout that was sent to Westlandia had not yet returned – but it was becoming apparent that they had plenty of help, so maybe this wasn't even necessary...**

"Phew!" exclaimed Sammi Jo. "I had no idea we could accomplish so much so fast! When do you think the battle will begin?"

"We are shooting for tomorrow morning. If we can catch Drakon by surprise, then we will have a much better chance of winning and saving our land!"

"Sounds good to us!" said Jake. "We will be here bright and early and by tomorrow night, your land will be safe!"

"That is very optimistic," Kirstin replied, "but, sounds like a great plan!"

After returning home, Sammi Jo finally had a chance to write to Kara and update her on everything that had been going on...

Dear Kara,

So much has been going on around here that I don't even know where to being! I wish we could talk, but I hope to see you soon, so you will be able to hear about all of this in person!

We are getting ready to defend Edenlandia against a dragon named Drakon and some evil cuttlefish that transform into sea dragons!

The entire ocean has come together to help us! It was amazing to swim with dolphins, whales, sharks, sea turtles... and many more!

I am going to have siblings! (fingers crossed). We are waiting to hear back from the adoption agency – so soon hopefully!

Just in case you forgot, my birthday is in a few days. I was hoping that we could make some plans for you to be here! Wouldn't that be fun?

Love, Sammi Jo

12

The Day of the Battle

Sammi Jo's dad greeted them both at the breakfast table to confirm that he talked to the school in New York. Not only had they agreed to add two new children to their roster, he had made arrangements for Riley to stay in the same room with Sammi Jo and Kara AND had gotten them to agree to having a dog for a mascot. Jack would be able to stay with Jase, and Jase would have to be responsible for his care, but as a "mascot," he would be expected to attend all the school events and wear a vest with the school crest on it!

It seemed as if everything was moving along and Sammi Jo could hardly contain her excitement, however, they needed to get to the beach – today was a big day for Edenlandia also and they had some pretty major commitments that they needed to handle today!

Screech was waiting for them as they approached the beach. He seemed to be pretty tense and not wanting to talk much, but since Sammi Jo and Jake were feeling the same, there were no hurt feelings.

He swam quickly and quietly to the gates of Edenlandia where the swarms of sea life and the people of Edenlandia were silently gathered.

"Welcome Screech, Sammi Jo, and Jake!" announced Kirstin quietly. "We have decided that we will all head out to the trench and quietly gather around to see what happens. We hope that there will be a peaceful resolution to this problem, but we have to be prepared, just in case."

"I agree!" stated Sammi Jo vehemently. "I don't want to see anyone get hurt! I even don't want to see Drakon or Tekoah get hurt."

"None of us do!" agreed Cody. "We have the cannon working and the swords ready, just in the need arises, but I have never hurt anyone or anything in my life, and I certainly don't want to start today..."

Hundreds and hundreds of heads nodded in agreement and they all began to move slowly toward the trench, as if they were all of one mind.

The closer they came to the trench, the slower and quieter they all became. This was not something anyone wanted to do – they only wanted to defend their land and get to the bottom of Drakon' s hard feelings and how he managed to get Tekoah to side with him!

They finally arrived at the clearing before the trench. The ghost parrots floated silently over to report that they had heard nothing from the trench all morning.

"We don't know what is going on!" stated Minnie. "Perhaps they have gone..."

It was super hard to see in the dark, but within moments the lanternfish began to appear in pin pricks over the edge of the trench. They formed a huge circle of light around all the new arrivals.

Sammi Jo heaved a huge sigh of relief as she loudly thanked all the lanternfish for coming to give them some light.

Fighting a battle, or even having a conversation was impossible when you couldn't see each other!

It seemed like hours that they all stood or floated silently waiting for something to happen. The mammals, such as the dolphins and the orcas, disappeared occasionally to go to the surface for a breath of air, but other than that, there was very little movement.

When it appeared that nothing was going to happen today, Drakon suddenly appeared over the side of the trench. His eyes were wild and red and he had smoke and fire coming out of his nose and mouth.

He glared at them in silence as one by one a small band of cuttlefish appeared over the side of the trench to stand silently beside him.

There were still no words spoken as Tekoah and Saqua finally appeared and positioned themselves in front of Drakon and the cuttlefish. Tekoah was brandishing a huge, shiny sword. His silvery colored hair floated around his head and he looked completely wild. Definitely not the Tekoah that the people of Edenlandia remembered!

"Why have you all come here?" Drakon boomed out at long last.

Kirstin and Cody, the leaders of Edenlandia, moved forward to speak with Drakon.

"We have received word that you are planning an attack against our land." stated Kirstin firmly. "And we are here to defend our people and our beloved kingdom!"

"And how would you have heard such a thing?" asked Tekoah. "There is no one here who would have relayed such a story."

"We have our ways," stated Cody firmly, "and we want to know what has caused this and why you would want to do such a thing to your family!"

"The people of Edenlandia are NOT my family," stated Tekoah vehemently. "You all made that clear during the gathering so many years ago. No one wanted me around, no one wanted to be my friend and when I chose the different path, no one tried to stop me."

"But, Tekoah," explained Kirstin, "Everyone has that choice – we don't stand in the way of someone who chooses differently. We did not expect you to leave. You did that of your own accord."

"No one tried to stop me!" Tekoah said with defiance. "If anyone had acted like they cared, perhaps I would've stayed..."

"It's too bad you felt that way," said Cody, "If you would have just talked to us, we could've explained. None of knew how you felt."

"ENOUGH TALK!" screamed Drakon. "We have all been hurt by the people of Edenlandia and we will know take revenge upon the people that destroyed our lives and our families!"

All the cuttlefish immediately transformed in fire breathing sea dragons and began to slowly approach the large gathering of sea creatures.

Cody ran to the ship to the prepare the cannon for attack. All the merpeople that had swords, held them up in a preparation for battle and the sharks began to swarm towards the dragons.

"Wait!" screamed Sammi Jo as she held up her arms. "Why are you all so angry about something that happened so long ago? Drakon, not one person or creature here was alive when your sister went missing. How can you blame them for something that happened so long ago?"

"If it weren't for the people of Edenlandia, my family would still be together. I would not be the only sea dragon left in the ocean and perhaps we would've have been able to grow our population."

"But this makes no sense," stated Jake firmly. "WE and the others here, were not even alive when your family issues began. How is it possible that you can blame them?"

"I CAN and I WILL!" yelled Drakon. "It doesn't matter to me that it all happened so long ago, I am still angry and there is no one else for me to blame. It may have been the Edenlandia of old, but I will take my vengeance upon you so that you can feel the way I felt back then."

With this he and the transformed cuttlefish came rushing forward with flames shooting out of their mouths.

The leatherbacks quickly positioned themselves in front of the group with their backs facing the flames as a shield against the fire.

The sharks and dolphins swam close and began to batter the dragons with their noses, hoping to push them back over the trench.

Tekoah raced towards the closest merman and they began battling with their swords. Tekoah had obviously been practicing and began to quickly wear down the merman, others with swords raced quickly to help, but Tekoah and Saqua held their ground. They never seemed to tire, and the sword fight continued.

The cannon finally boomed, and a huge cannonball landed in the middle of the clearing spraying sand and huge plumes of water over everyone. No one was hurt, but the spray did manage to put out the dragons flames for a short period of time.

This allowed everyone a moment to breathe as they could stop defending themselves against the flames and the leatherbacks got to relax for a moment and cool off their backs.

Throughout it all, Kirstin, Jake and the ghost parrots, were trying to figure out something they could say that would appease Drakon and Tekoah. Something that would help them to see that what happened long ago, had no bearing on today, and that if they could just talk about their differences, perhaps we could solve this without any more violence.

As the flames began again, Drakon came forward with a vengeance. The cuttlefish gang was taking longer to regain their flames so were holding back.

The swordfight was continuing so no one seemed to notice the new visitors until they were upon us...

13

The Reunion

Into the midst of the battle rode King Richard, Queen Alicia, and King William, from Westlandia. The scout had found them and brought them back to help.

King Richard, the oldest one of the group, held up his hand to momentarily stop the battle.

"Drakon!" he announced loudly. "This battle is outrageous! None of the people of this land have anything to do with the loss of your family. This all happened even before I was born! If you remember the story, it was a couple of sea dragons who caused the quarrels in the first place."

"That is not the way I remember it," stated Drakon stubbornly. "Your people banished my sister's new friends. This is what caused the battle that caused

Kyree to disappear and my two brothers, Zurka and Lyzer, to be killed."

"Because...," stated Queen Alicia. "They were wreaking havoc upon our land and people. They were not banished for no good reason, they were banished because they were up to no good!"

"Again..." said Drakon, "NOT the way I remember it. It is your kind that caused me to lose my family, it is YOU who caused Tekoah to leave Edenlandia. He came to me as he knew that I would understand what it meant to be an outcast and different from the others. It is our turn to make you feel bad, as we have felt for so long!"

"First of all," said King William, "We had no idea that Tekoah was feeling left out. He should have talked to us or his family about it."

"Secondly, we had nothing to do with your family, Drakon! We are simply the descendants of the people you are so angry and... and thirdly..." he stopped and peered into the distance. His eyes getting wider with each second that passed.

As everyone turned to look, the dark shapes in the distance began to get larger and larger...

"Wow! Would you look at that!" exclaimed Sammi Jo loudly. "It looks like more sea dragons!"

Everyone tensed, thinking that the battle was now going to get more intense. The shadows in the distance continued to get closer, when Drakon's flames went out and he began to get tears in his eyes.

"It's Kyree." He muttered in a small and quiet voice. "It's Kyree!"

All of the fight went out of him as he rushed over to meet Kyree, Maximus, and several smaller sea dragons.

"You're alive!" he said with wonder.

"Yes, we are alive," smiled Kyree back at him. "And, as you can see, you have some nieces and nephews you need to get to know!"

For the next hour, they listened to Kyree and Maximus's stories about what had happened after the original battle.

Once they realized that Zurka and Lyzer had been killed, they decided to disappear knowing that Drakon would never forgive them for allowing that to happen and for causing the ruckus in the first place.

Maximus's brother, Lurko, had been badly injured and had died of his wounds a short time later. This left Kyree and Maximus alone and unsure of what to do. Although, Kyree, had been very sad, they had decided to move far, far away so they wouldn't hurt anyone ever again. They had no idea that they were hurting everyone worse by staying away, then if they had faced the problems in the first place.

They had eventually decided to start a family and time had gotten away from them. When word had reached them of the battle and that Drakon was the reason – they decided it was finally time to return to Edenlandia and put an end to Drakon's stories.

"Drakon," said Kyree. "I am so very sorry to have caused you so much grief over the years. I wish it could've been different, but I was afraid to face you. It was my fault for bring Lurko and Maximus here. It is they who caused all of the grief and it is they who deserved to be banished for what they did to the people of Edenlandia. Please forgive them. As you can see, Maximus and I are quite happy, we have beautiful children and have tried hard to forget the troubles of the past."

Drakon and Kyree hugged and then Kyree introduced Drakon to his three new nieces and nephews.

Maximus came forward to apologize to everyone.

"I am aware that my brother and myself are the ones responsible for all of the turmoil we caused years ago and this newest problem, as well. I would like to ask for your forgiveness. I was young and had never had the loving family that many of you have and make some bad decisions. I now have a beautiful family and regret all of the bad decisions I made in the past. Please accept my apologies!"

Everyone cheered! Swords and cannons were put away. The cuttlefish dragons turned back into cuttlefish and everyone began to talk at once about the great outcome!

Drakon stepped forward at this point.

"I, too, must apologize," he stated, "I was blaming the wrong people for everything that happened so long ago. I am pleased to have my sister back and a whole new family to go along with her! It has definitely turned out to be the Best Day Ever, as Sammi Jo would say."

Tekoah had been standing aside saying nothing. He and Saqua had not been acknowledged and he still considered himself to be an outcast.

An older mercouple swam up to him at about that time and silently hugged him. They said nothing, just put their arms around him and hugged. Tears began to stream down their faces as Saqua's parents also appeared.

No words seemed to be necessary as the two families hugged, laughed and cried. All the troubles of the past seemed to disappear as everyone rejoiced in the reunion of all three of the families!

The royal family of Edenlandia gathered together in a huddle and then King Richard rose up to make an announcement.

"We, the people of Edenlandia, would like to invite Drakon and his family to move back to the caves outside the kingdom. The caves in which the sea dragons had occupied for centuries when we were all friends. They have sat empty for too long and we would love to have the full of laughter again."

Everyone cheered and Drakon and Kyree accepted gratefully.

"And," he continued, "we would love to make an exception for Tekoah and Saqua. For the first time ever, we would like to have Tekoah and Saqua "re-choose". If you would like to come back to our kingdom and, once again, be part of our annual gathering, you simply need to say the word!"

Tekoah and Saqua glanced at each other and then with big smiles, accepted gratefully.

Kirstin, hurriedly, gathered up some sea coral and vines to make a necklace, motioned Tekoah and Saqua to come forward and solemnly placed one over each of their heads.

The crowds cheered wildly as Tekoah hopped on Saqua's back and they made a victory circle amidst the applause and cheers of the people.

"You see," stated Jake proudly. "I told you it would all be over by the end of the day!"

The sea creatures began to disperse back to their parts of the ocean. Ready for life to resume as normal.

Arkeo, however, rushed over to Sammi Jo and Jake to announce that he had decided to make his home outside of Edenlandia, so he could remain friends with them, Screech, and all the new friends he had made.

All in all, it was an epic battle and an epic good ending to a very long and ancient story! And, as Sammi Jo would say ...

The Best Adventure Ever!

But, it hadn't ended yet ...

By the time they arrived back at Edenlandia, things seemed a little weird. Many of the others had left before them, but the whole land seemed very quiet.

Sammi Jo thought that there would be laughter and celebration, and was surprised at the quietness that surrounded her.

"What is going on?" asked Sammi Jo in a hushed tone. "Where is everyone?"

"I don't know," replied Screech in an odd voice. "Let's go to the big cave and see if anyone is there."

Screech and Jake exchanged glances and then quickly looked away as they swam up to the big cave.

Something is up, thought Sammi Jo to herself, but why are they hiding it from me?

"SURPRISE!" yelled EVERYONE as they swam through the entrance of the big cave.

The entire town had gathered together to wish Sammi Jo Happy Birthday! With all of the battle preparations, it was astonishing that they would have had the time to think about this, much less plan a party!

"We wanted one of our very favorite human beings to know how much we love her and appreciate her!" said Margo as she came rushing up to give Sammi Jo a gorgeous birthday crown made of sea shells, pearls and the amazing little gems from the sea walls.

"I am so surprised!" exclaimed Sammi Jo. "I didn't even know that you all knew that my birthday was tomorrow!"

"Jake told us," said Dafne with a smile. "It was super hard to keep the secret, and we were so worried that it wouldn't happen, with the battle and all... anyway, it has all turned out great! Were you really surprised?"

"Absolutely!" replied Sammi Jo. "It never even crossed my mind!"

Tons of food was laid out, a great cake made of... well made of stuff that cakes are usually made from, and another table piled high with birthday presents.

Arkeo showed up with his adorable little turtle smile with some presents of his own and before too long, Drakon, Kyree and her family, also joined the excitement.

It was the most surprised Sammi Jo had ever been and it her birthday wasn't even until tomorrow. What could possibly top this?

All too soon it was time to go. Sammi Jo hugged everyone and thanked everyone and told them all how it had been the Best Day Ever, as they all laughed and rolled her eyes. Everyone in the WHOLE OCEAN seemed to know that was Sammi Jo's favorite expression when she was happy!

Screech returned them to the surface and promised to see them in a couple of days. They all figured that there would be some big plans with the family tomorrow, so decided to wait until the next day to journey back to Edenlandia and all their new friends.

"Happy Birthday!" he hollered right before he dove under the water. "See you soon!"

14

Sammi Jo's Birthday Surprise

Sammi Jo, as usual, lay in bed the next morning thinking about everything that had happened the day before and the amazing reunion and the awesome surprise party!

She threw herself out of bed as she realized that TODAY was really her birthday!

Hugging her stuffed animals and dancing around the room, shouting,

"Today is my Birthday! I am NINE years old TODAY!"

She went running out of her room to pound on Jake's door.

"Get up! Get up!"

"Go away, I don't feel good," he groaned through the closed door.

"But, today is..."

"Go away!"

Sammi Jo shook her head and bounded down the stairs. *How could he forget what day it is? After that huge party yesterday, there was no way he could have forgotten... Oh well, her parents would remember!*

Her mom was rushing into her office as Sammi Jo reached the bottom of the stairs.

"Morning!" she said to her mom excitedly.

"Oh, hi honey!" said Mrs. Meriwether distractedly. "Cereal is on the table if you are hungry – I have to get to work, I just got a call from my publisher and they have moved up my deadline. No time to talk!"

"But... well, where is Dad?" Sammi Jo questioned in a small voice.

"Oh, he had to go to town early today. He will be back before dinner. Just run off and play, you can see him later."

Her mother disappeared into her office and shut the door and Sammi Jo stepped sadly into the kitchen to eat her cold breakfast.

How could they all forget? This has never happened before. What the heck is going on?

Well, she was not going to let this get her down, after all, she had a great party yesterday. Maybe she would just go to the beach by herself and hope that Screech showed up. Or maybe Arkeo...

She gathered up her backpack and a book, just in case no one showed up and headed down to the beach. It seemed just like it did at the beginning of the summer when she was looking for a new friend and was spending her days on the beach alone. It just seemed odd that it was happening on her birthday!

There was no one at the beach when she got there, so she spread out her blanket under the tree, plopped herself down and began to read.

She had been reading for a couple of hours when she heard a noise coming from the water and glanced up quickly.

Nothing... nobody had come to see her, but then... she saw something at the water's edge.

She quickly put down her book and ran to see what it was.

Odd, she thought to herself. Where did this come from? It looked just like one of the ancient tablets from the cave.

She glanced toward the ocean again for a clue and swore that she saw Echo peering at her, but she looked again, he was gone. Perhaps Echo had placed the tablet here.

As she turned it over, she saw the writing that had been etched on the back side of the tablet:

It's your Birthday! Shouldn't you be getting home? Your party is going to start Without you!

They didn't forget! Jake must have been planning this all along. After all, her parents wouldn't have known about the tablets!

She quickly glanced toward the ocean again, but seeing nothing, gathered up her stuff, and went running towards home!

There were several cars in the driveway and she could smell wood smoke coming from somewhere, so she assumed that her dad was home, and had started the bonfire.

She flew through the kitchen and out the back to see a ton of people at the beach behind the house!

"SURPRISE! SURPRISE!" they all shouted!

Sammi Jo stopped in stunned surprise at all the people she had not expected to see.

Kara and her parents were there! Beau (the boy from the adventure) and his parents were there. Jake's parents and little brother were there. And even Mr. Schermerhorn from the shop in town!

Standing a little to the side was Mrs. Gilmore, holding hands tightly with a tall boy and a girl with

jet black pigtails! Standing patiently beside them was a white boxer dog!

Kara came running up to throw her arms around her!

"Oh my gosh! It has been so hard not to write back to you! All of your stuff sounds so amazing that I can't even believe it! But, I knew if I wrote you back, I would spill the beans – so here I am!"

"This is so great! I figured you were just busy, but I am super excited you are here!"

Kara took her hand and drug her over to where Mrs. Gilmore was standing. Mr. and Mrs. Meriwether came up to join them, as well.

"Hi, Sammi Jo!" said Mrs. Gilmore. "I would like to introduce you to your potential new brother and sister, oh and by the way, Happy Birthday!"

Jase and Riley seemed pretty quiet, but Sammi Jo knew that wouldn't last long as she grabbed them both by the hands and dragged them across the beach to meet everyone else. The dog, Jack, bounded along with them, with a big old dog smile on his droopy boxer face. He was certainly a happy dog!

Mrs. Gilmore and Sammi Jo's parents, along with the other parents that were there, watched smilingly as all the children played happily together, building sandcastles, throwing sticks into the water for the dog, and skipping stones.

It certainly seemed as if Jase and Riley were going to fit right in!

After a while, Sammi Jo came running back up to her parent's side.

"I thought everyone had forgotten my birthday," she panted. "But, it has turned out to be the Best Birthday Ever! How did you pull this all off?"

"We had a lot of help from Jake," they replied laughingly. "He is the one who figured out how to get you out of the house, and then how to get you to get back at the right time! We don't exactly know what he did, but he said he would get a message to you in time."

"Well, that he did!" said Sammi Jo with delight.

And then turning to Mrs. Gilmore.

"What do you think? Do you think they like us? Can they stay?"

"I would say that it seems that they are having a great time and the chances are pretty good! I will talk with them in a little while and we will let you know!" she replied with a big grin on her face.

"WOO HOO!" shouted Sammi Jo as she went running back down the beach to join the other children.

"I must say," said Mrs. Gilmore. "I'm not sure I have ever met a child that is so exuberant about everything!"

"That she is," her parents replied with a fond smile. "And has a heart of gold!" they added on quickly.

The rest of the day went quickly as Sammi Jo's dad continued to feed the bonfire and hand out marshmallows to all of the willing hands.

Soon it was time for dinner. The parents gathered up all the food from the house and brought it down to the "starving" children. They roasted their hotdogs and corn on the cob, made some banana boats, (which are hollowed out bananas filled with chocolate and marshmallows, wrapped in foil and placed in the fire to melt), and then sang campfire songs while they were waiting for the banana boats to get ready.

Jase and Riley seemed super happy, which made Sammi Jo, her parents and Mrs. Gilmore really happy!

"I have never had such a fun day in my entire life!" said Riley excitedly.

"Me, neither," mumbled Jase with his mouth full of banana boat goo.

"So," said Mrs. Gilmore, "would you like to spend the night tonight? We can talk about all the future plans tomorrow."

"Yes!" shouted Jase, Riley, and Sammi Jo all at the same time.

Everyone laughed, and it was agreed that Jase and Riley would spend the night and get to know their possible new family a little bit better.

Beau and his family and Mr. Schermerhorn and Mrs. Gilmore headed back to town, but Kara's family and Jake's family were staying, so they all headed back to the house and began to prepare sleeping arrangements for everyone.

This was the Best Birthday and the Best Adventure ever!

15

The New Kids Meet Screech

It had been two days since Sammi Jo's birthday and so much had happened that is was hard to remember it all!

Kara's parents had left, but Kara had stayed. They would meet up when they were all moving back to school.

Jake and his family had left with plans to meet up for Christmas... maybe...

Mrs. Gilmore had come back the day after Sammi Jo's birthday party. Jase and Riley had made the decision that this was the BEST family they could ever have hoped for and the paperwork had been signed. Mrs. Gilmore promised to come and visit as much as possible as she had grown very fond of the entire Meriwether family!

And now, it was time to introduce Jase, Riley, and Kara, to Screech, Arkeo, and the people of Edenlandia.

Tomorrow was the day they needed to head back to New York, so this was it for this summer...

Sammi Jo was kind of sad as they all headed down the beach because she knew this would be the last time she could see everyone this summer, but figured they would work something out...

So, now they were standing on the beach waiting. Jase was much like Jake in that he didn't really believe any of the stories, but Riley and Kara totally believed and were eagerly waiting and watching.

It didn't take long to catch a glimpse of Screech appearing around the side of the rock.

The girls squealed with delight, while Jase simply stood there with his mouth open!

"Hello!" squealed Screech in his amazing high and squealy voice.

"OMG!!" said Jase. "I can't believe this is really happening. How did I get so lucky – I totally love my new life!"

Sammi Jo had already grown to love her new brother and sister and gazed at him fondly.

"I told you it was true!" she said with a smirk. "Maybe, in time, you will come to believe the things I say!"

"I guess I have no choice now!" he replied with a laugh.

Sammi Jo waved at Screech. They searched for more translators on the beach and he threw four more scales at her for breathing devices for Kara, Jase, Riley, and Jack. They had to figure out something special for Jack, as they certainly couldn't leave him behind. But, they got it handled and Sammi Jo showed them how to put everything on, explained what they were for and they all waded out into the water to get on Screech's back.

The super cool part of all of this, is that with the translators, they could talk with Jack too!

This would be the first of many more great adventures to come for the new Meriwether kids and it would be EPIC, they all knew!

Excited to see what's coming next?

Keep an eye out for Sammi Jo's next adventure in Book 4 of the Sammi Jo Adventure Series:

Sammi Jo and the Best Christmas Ever!

Previous books in the Sammi Jo Adventure Series:

Book 1 – Sammi Jo and the Best Day Ever!
Book 2 – Sammi Jo and the Best Rodeo Ever!
Book 3 – Sammi Jo and the Best Adventure Ever!

81391952R00086

Made in the USA
Columbia, SC
30 November 2017